FR - '59̃/ss

The Big Ugly Monster

and the
Little Stone Rabbit

To Pete and Mike

THE BIG UGLY MONSTER AND THE LITTLE STONE RABBIT
A JONATHAN CAPE BOOK 0 224 07003 7

Published in Great Britain by Jonathan Cape,
an imprint of Random House Children's Books

This edition published 2004

1 3 5 7 9 10 8 6 4 2

RANDOM HOUSE CHILDREN'S BOOKS
61-63 Uxbridge Road, London W5 5SA
A division of The Random House Group Ltd

RANDOM HOUSE AUSTRALIA (PTY) LTD
20 Alfred Street, Milsons Point, Sydney,
New South Wales 2061, Australia
RANDOM HOUSE NEW ZEALAND LTD
18 Poland Road, Glenfield, Auckland 10, New Zealand
RANDOM HOUSE (PTY) LTD
Endulini, 5A Jubilee Road, Parktown 2193, South Africa

THE RANDOM HOUSE GROUP Limited Reg. No. 954009
www.kidsatrandomhouse.co.uk

A CIP catalogue record for this book is available from the British Library.

Printed and bound in Singapore

The Big Ugly Monster

and the
Little Stone Rabbit

Chris Wormell

A Tom Maschler Book

Jonathan Cape • London

Once, in a cave, there lived a big ugly monster. Perhaps the ugliest monster in the whole world.

This is the cave.

And in this picture the monster is just about to come out. So be careful when you turn the page.

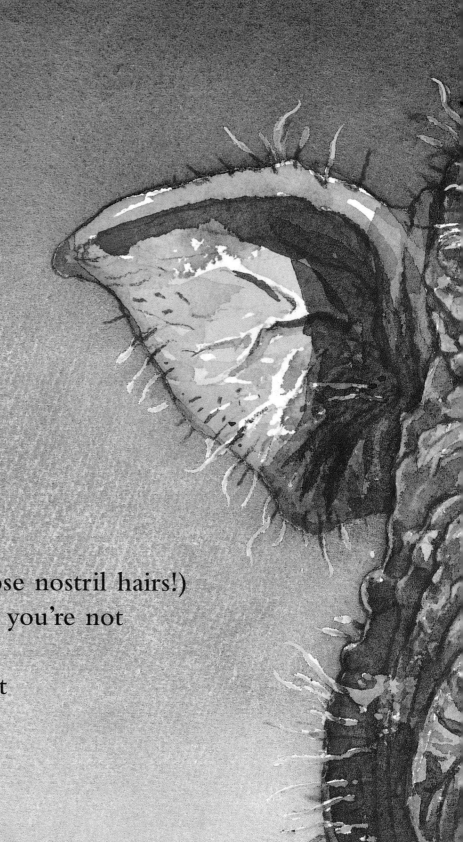

There he is.

Pretty ugly, eh? (Just look at those nostril hairs!)
Of course this is only a picture, so you're not
getting the whole effect.

You're not getting the ugliness at
full strength.

It was pretty powerful.

He was so ugly that all the animals and birds ran and flew away as soon as they saw him. He was so ugly that all the flowers dropped their petals and the trees shed their leaves and even the grass turned brown and withered and died.

He was so ugly that if he looked up at the blue sky on a sunny day it would most likely turn grey and pour with rain, or even snow.

He was so ugly that if he stepped into a pond for a swim it would instantly dry up with a hiss of steam. That's how ugly he was.

All around the monster's cave there was not a single living thing. It was such a sad and desolate place.

And do you know – the monster was sad and desolate too. For though he was horrible and ugly on the outside he wasn't on the inside. On the inside he was lonely. He just wanted someone to talk to.

But there was no one.

And so he talked to the rocks.

Then one day he had an idea.

He began to make stone animals from the rocks. He made a fox
and a badger and a deer and a bear and a tortoise and a rabbit.
    They weren't very good; at least, the heads weren't very good.
The monster had never seen much of the real animals' heads.
The back ends were better; that was the bit he usually saw
as the animals ran away.

When he had finished, the monster
was pleased with all his stone
animals, and he smiled.

Unfortunately the monster was so ugly that when he
smiled the stone animals cracked and shattered and he
was left with a pile of rubble.

All except one of the animals, that is.

The stone rabbit did not crack. Perhaps the rock was stronger.
I don't know why it was but the stone rabbit did not crack.

Even when the monster gave it an **extra big smile** just to test it, the stone rabbit did not crack.

So the monster talked to the stone rabbit and though the rabbit did not have much to say, the monster was happy.

The monster sang to the stone rabbit and when he sang, rocks would shatter and split for miles around.

And though the rabbit never joined in, not even for the chorus, still the monster was happy.

Sometimes, on nights when the moon was full, the
monster danced, and when he danced the ground shook
like an earthquake and great cracks split the land and
the moon dashed away and hid behind the clouds.
And though the rabbit never joined in, not even to
tap its foot, the monster was happy nonetheless.

Sometimes the monster did tricks. He stood on one hand and
juggled and did cartwheels and somersaults, and when he did
his tricks lightning flashed, thunder cracked, the wind howled

like a tornado and the rain lashed down. And though the rabbit never joined in, unless you count playing statues, the monster was happy nonetheless.

Years and years passed by and the monster talked
and sang and danced and did his tricks. But sometimes
they both just sat and watched the storms roll by.

And though the monster got older and older and uglier
and uglier and his hair turned grey and his teeth fell out,
the stone rabbit never changed at all.

A time came when the monster was so old he could no longer sing or dance or do tricks. He could still play draughts, however, and though the stone rabbit was a poor player – even when the monster suggested some very clever moves – he was happy nonetheless.

But one day the monster never came out
of his cave and the stone rabbit sat alone.

That very day the sun came out and green grass began to grow. Soon the flowers bloomed and vines scrambled over rocks and hung down over the mouth of the cave.

Trees grew up straight and tall and all the animals and birds came back. It was a beautiful place now, perhaps the most beautiful place in the whole world.

People would go there for picnics and admire the
views, and though they never took much notice
of the stone rabbit, they sometimes
wondered how it had got there.